Humbleton

Jayna Duckenfield

• Barnsley Ink •

Printed in the United States of America

ISBN 978-1-946425-28-7
Book Design by CSinclaire Write-Design
Book Cover by Austeja Slavickaite Wojtczak and Charlotte Sinclaire
Illustrations by Austeja Slavickaite Wojtczak

Barnsley Ink | Raleigh, NC
An imprint of Write Way Publishing Company

This book is dedicated to my father.

Thanks for believing in me
and always calling my writing a gift
instead of a hobby.
Without you, this book
wouldn't have happened.

Your Sweet Pea loves you, Daddy!

Chapter One

ONCE UPON A TIME, in a far away land, there was a kingdom named Arrogancia. In the land, there also was a very special purple pebble. This pebble, smaller than a child's fist and smooth as a river stone, was desired by all. Every knight, every duchess, every king and every queen, every shop owner, every farmer, every wife, mother, and daughter, well, really everyone desired to possess the purple pebble. Why? Because this was no ordinary pebble. It was magical. Stories were told that once every hundred years the pebble would appear and grant one true wish to someone somewhere in the land.

All of Arrogancia was filled with excitement. This was the year the purple pebble would appear, and the people were certain it would arrive in their kingdom this time.

And although they did not know it yet, they were right. The pebble had quietly arrived in Arrogancia and was hidden behind a bush in Clock Tower Square. It was listening to the excited talk of the inhabitants.

"I can't wait for the pebble to come. I'm sure I will be chosen. I'm going to wish to be the most famous knight in the land!" said one knight.

"What makes you think the pebble will choose you? I'm very beautiful," a duchess replied with a wave of her fan.

"Oh, no. Both of you are wrong! The pebble will certainly choose me. I mean...I am rich and powerful! I live in a huge house and own vast lands," boasted a wealthy farmer.

The pebble could not believe what it was

hearing. Did no one in this kingdom have good intentions? "If the people are going to act like this, I don't want to grant a wish to any of them. This just isn't right!" the pebble whispered. It longed for someone who was brave, honest, and had a good attitude. And so it was that the pebble made a decision. The pebble resolved not to reveal its location except to someone of noble character.

With that, there was a loud *DOOONG!* The chime signifying the pebble's arrival rang throughout Arrogancia. All the people shouted and ran to Clock Tower Square, since the traditional place where the pebble appeared to grant wishes was always the local town square. But when the people arrived, there was no pebble waiting for them. Murmurs of "Where is it?" and "What's going on?" were heard coming from the crowd.

Suddenly, the sky grew dark, and there was a great clap of thunder. The crowd gasped as lighting struck the ground. The people were stunned until someone said, "Well, if the pebble is not going to come to us, then we must go to it! Whoever finds the pebble first gets the wish!" With loud cheers, everyone scattered. The search was on!

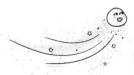

Chapter Two

NO ONE FOUND THE purple pebble the first day, though they searched high and low throughout the city. The pebble just wasn't to be found. Tomorrow they would begin their search outside the city. Finally, as it grew dark, everyone went home feeling discouraged. Everyone that is except Sir Liesalot. He would stop at nothing until he found the pebble. In fact, he wanted to find the pebble so much that he slinked back to Clock Tower Square, climbed the clock tower, and turned the hands on the big chiming clock back two hours so he could get a head start on everyone in the morning.

And that wasn't all. He even put up two signs that said "Road Closed" and another one that said "Detour" that led to a dead end. Sir Liesalot loved to play, but he wasn't very good at playing fair. The next morning, when the majority of the people of Arrogancia were still sleeping because the clock had yet to chime, Sir Liesalot slipped out of town to begin his search of the countryside.

He walked and walked, checking behind every tree and every bush he passed. "Where are you, pebble? You've got to be around here somewhere," Sir Liesalot called. He threw his hands in the air and knocked some berries off of a nearby bush. Little did he know, hiding behind the bush was a fierce beast. It had the head of a lion with blazing eyes and a body with the thick, wooly fur of a bear. But when the beast jumped out from the bush with a roar, it made Sir Liesalot laugh. The roar sounded more squeaky than scary. The laughter made the beast angry, so it charged Sir Liesalot.

But Sir Liesalot wasn't fazed. He drew his sword and began to battle the beast. Showing no fear and with a few swift moves, Sir Liesalot had the beast running through the woods in no time and was ready to continue on with his quest.

"Come out, come out, wherever you are. I know you're here somewhere, little peb...," Sir Liesalot sang. Something caught Sir Liesalot's eye. Resting near a tree only a few feet away was a treasure chest, opened wide, full of golden coins. *Well, well, I wonder whose gold this is*, Sir Liesalot thought to himself. *Maybe since no one is around, I can take a few pieces and no one will ever know.*

Then Sir Liesalot noticed the name *King Noble* carved on the chest. "Hmm...I should probably return this to the King, but I really want a few coins," Sir Liesalot muttered. "There are so many things I could buy with gold coins!" After a few seconds, Sir Liesalot decided he would take just a few coins. If

anyone asked about the chest, he would say he hadn't seen it.

He stuffed a few gold coins in his sleeves and continued on his way, looking high and low for the pebble. Soon Sir Liesalot saw a young servant.

"Excuse me, sir," said the boy. "Have you seen King Noble's chest? It appears to have fallen out of our caravan on the way back to the castle."

Sir Liesalot could feel the gold coins in his sleeves. With a smooth smile, he replied, "No, I haven't seen the chest, and I've been walking for a while. In fact, you probably want to turn around and go in the opposite direction. It's definitely not on the road I traveled." Sir Liesalot gave a nod as the young servant ran away in the opposite direction.

Sir Liesalot's dishonesty did not serve him well. As soon as he took his second step to continue his quest, a giant net dropped from the sky and trapped him.

"Hey, what's going on?" shouted Sir Liesalot. "Let me out! Let me out!"

In a blink, the net lifted him into the air and whisked him right back to Clock Tower Square. It rather rudely dumped him in the middle of the square and disappeared. In a huff, Sir Liesalot tried his best to resume his journey, but he was unable to move from the spot where he landed. He shifted his body to the left and then to the right, but nothing seemed to work. His feet simply would not budge. "Help! Help!" he cried. But everyone in the city was out searching for the pebble, so there was no one to hear his cries.

After a while, a pirate came strolling by and spotted Sir Liesalot, stuck tight and unable to move.

"Argh! What be the problem, sir?" asked the pirate.

"I'm stuck!" Sir Liesalot puffed out his chest a bit and said, "I'm Sir Liesalot, and I'm in search of the purple pebble hidden

somewhere in our kingdom, but now I can't move from this spot. I was walking along, minding my own business, when all of a sudden, this net dropped from the sky, captured me, and brought me here. Can you help me?"

"Hmm," said the pirate. "So, you were just walking along the road and the net dropped out of nowhere?"

Sir Liesalot frowned. He knew that he hadn't told the truth.

"Not exactly...," confessed Sir Liesalot. "I took a few of King Noble's gold coins from a lost chest I found, and then I sort of, well, I guess you'd say, lied to one of his servants when he asked me if I'd seen the chest."

The pirate nodded. He did not approve of Sir Liesalot's lie, but as a pirate, he knew the lure of gold. Still, he did not want to leave the man trapped forever.

"I really want to find the pebble, and I know I shouldn't have lied," said Sir Liesalot miserably.

"Aye. I have heard of such a pebble, and if I'm not mistaken, whoever receives the pebble gets one true wish," the pirate said.

"Yes, that's the legend," replied Sir Liesalot.

"Well, sir, I will do my best to find this pebble and wish for you to be free," the pirate said. Luckily for Sir Liesalot, this pirate liked to help people. Of course, the pirate enjoyed the thrill when he happened to find treasure, but he often would give away whatever he found. The thing Sir Liesalot didn't know, however, was that this pirate was sort of lazy.

"Oh, thank you so much!" Sir Liesalot said happily.

And with that, the pirate set out to find the purple pebble.

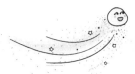

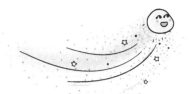

Chapter Three

NOW THE PIRATE WAS only stopping at a port near the edge of Arrogancia to stock up on supplies. He and his crew were in search of a certain flower in one of the kingdom's forests. The pirate should have stopped weeks ago for supplies, but he had been too lazy to make port. He and his crew had been eating nothing but stale crackers for two weeks. "I shouldn't be gone long. I'm sure my first mate will get the supplies we need, and the crew can handle everything on the ship," the pirate muttered to himself.

As he walked along, the pirate made sure

to pay close attention to his surroundings just in case the pebble might pop up somewhere. At least he tried to pay close attention. He looked to the right and to the left, up and down, but all he saw were trees. Instead of walking further, the pirate sat down on a sturdy log. He was tired of looking already. "Argh! How can I find a pebble in all these trees!" the pirate complained.

He nearly fell off the log when he heard a voice call out to him. It was Sir Liesalot. "Keep going! You said you would find the pebble and wish me free!"

The pirate let out a deep sigh, stood up, and walked farther down the road until he could no longer hear Sir Liesalot's voice. After he had walked a while, he saw something shiny up ahead. As he got closer, he realized he had found the pieces of gold Sir Liesalot had stolen. The knight must have lost them when he was captured by the net.

Knowing that taking the gold was how Sir

Liesalot got himself into trouble, the pirate picked up the pieces and went to find the missing chest. The pirate wanted to take the gold, especially because he didn't have to do work to find it, but he knew there would be consequences.

"Hmm...I should try to find King Noble," the pirate said. "I can return the chest, and maybe the king can give me a clue about where the pebble might be!" Liking this idea, the pirate searched until he found the chest under the tree where Sir Liesalot had left it. He closed the chest and, with a heave, lifted it and began walking down the road once again, hoping to find King Noble's castle.

To pass the time, the pirate began to sing.

"With adventure on our backs,
Across the seven seas we sail.
Our ship, she's called The Belly Acher
Yo ho! Yo ho! Yo ho!
To the wind we wail!"

By the time the pirate had finished his song, he'd reached a fork in the road. To the left, there was a sign that had a picture of a sun on it, and to the right, there was a sign with a picture of a rain cloud.

"Argh! Where be me map when I need it?" the pirate grumbled. He didn't know which road to choose. "Well, I've been on the open seas enough to know that rain might not be a good thing," said the pirate. So, he chose left and walked down the road of sunshine.

Everything started off fine, but then the pirate heard a loud *"Screeeeeeech! C-Caw!"*

"Shiver me timbers! What was that?" The pirate looked up and down and all around. He saw nothing but a beautiful, golden, hot sun and an empty road.

"Screeeeeeech! C-Caw!" He heard the sound again, but it was louder this time. The pirate turned around, and that's when he saw them. Sun birds. These birds were native to Arrogancia and only lived in the part of

the land where it never rains. Their feathers thrive in the sun. If it's too cold, they get sticky, and it becomes hard for the sun birds to fly. Usually, the birds are peaceable, but there's one thing that makes them wild— gold! In the presence of gold, the sun birds' golden yellow wings turn black, and they let out horrible shrieks.

The pirate didn't know much about sun birds, but he knew that he had to protect the gold. He set King Noble's chest on the ground and drew his sword. As the birds swooped down to snatch the gold, the pirate's blade flashed back and forth while he dodged the creatures' sharp beaks. The faster his sword cut the air, the more annoyed the birds became until they flew away, shrieking as they went.

"Phew! That was a close one!" the pirate exhaled, trying to catch his breath. He wiped the sweat from his brow. "I need water! I had better find King Noble's castle soon!"

Taking a deep breath, the pirate picked

up the chest and began walking again. The left path that the pirate had chosen was the most desert-like place in Arrogancia. There was no trace of rain in this part of the land nor were there any trees to provide shade. Only cactus plants and small bushes grew there. "It's so hot! Why aren't there any trees? Where is the shade? Why did I even start on this quest?" His voice was gradually becoming quite whiny.

The chest of gold felt heavier and heavier, and the hotter he got, the more he complained. "Argh! I shouldn't even be here! It's not *my* fault that Sir Liesalot was captured by a net! It's too hot for this. I don't even know if I'm going the right way!" After a while, the pirate saw a few trees in the distance but instead of being happy about that, he plopped down on the ground and threw a tantrum. He was almost out of the desert, but he was too lazy to keep going.

"Arrrrgh! I have so much farther to walk! It's so hot. This chest is so heavy. I'm all sweaty. I'm hungry. I need wa...," he grumbled. But

the pirate's words were cut off. Before he could finish his last bellyache, a net fell from the sky, captured him, and in a blink, planted him in a spot right next to Sir Liesalot!

"What happened?" Sir Liesalot asked, both confused and upset. The pirate just shook his head, sweat still dripping. He had proved himself brave fighting the sun birds, but he could not stop complaining.

"I'm sorry, matey. It seems that me bellyachin' got the best of me," said the pirate sadly. "Now I'm stuck too! What will my crew do without me?"

Sir Liesalot let out a deep sigh. "I guess we'll just have to wait for someone else to come along," he said.

"Argh! I suppose you be right," the pirate said.

Before long, the two captives heard a loud, "Boogity Boogity Boo! I'm a troll in Arrogancia, and I'm gunna scare you!" Walking toward Sir Liesalot and the pirate was a small red and blue stripped troll. Noticing that Sir Liesalot and the pirate seemed unable to move, the troll stopped to see what was going on.

"What are you two doing just standing there? Shouldn't you be searching for the purple pebble?" The troll flashed a smirk, showing some pretty sharp teeth in the process.

"We can't move. We each set out to find the pebble but were only able to get so far before a giant net caught us and brought us back here," the pirate replied.

"Oh? A net caught you, you say. And why do you suppose that happened?" the troll asked.

Sir Liesalot hung his head and said, "Well, I was dishonest and stole some of King Noble's gold, and..."

"I complained far too much—about a lot of things," the pirate finished.

"Could you help us?" Sir Liesalot and the pirate asked in unison. On any other day, under any other circumstance, neither the

pirate nor Sir Liesalot would have asked the troll for help. Trolls of Arrogancia are known for being extremely selfish and jealous of their possessions. That's why their red fur is accompanied by *green* stripes.

The troll stared at Sir Liesalot and the pirate thoughtfully and gave a tug on his quite large nose before he finally answered.

"Well, boys, it's your lucky day. I'm in an extremely generous mood and have decided to help you. Besides, I have nothing else to do today. Everyone in the land is so focused on finding this pebble, there's no one around to scare."

"Oh, thank you so much!" exclaimed Sir Liesalot.

"Argh! Yes, thank ye," said the pirate. "Just make sure you're careful. This net is nothing to play with." Sir Liesalot nodded his head in agreement.

"Boys, boys, boys…," the troll chuckled. "You have nothing to worry about. I'll be back before you know it!" The troll gave a little bow to Sir Liesalot and the pirate, took a running start, and did back flips until he was out of sight.

"I sure hope he knows what he's doing," Sir Liesalot said.

Chapter Four

OF COURSE, SIR LIESALOT and the pirate were a little bit worried that the troll would be selfish and keep the pebble for himself, but at this point, they were willing to take the risk. However, Sir Liesalot and the pirate were so focused on wanting to be free that they hadn't noticed that this troll's stripes were *blue* and red and not *green* and red. Although he visited quite often, this troll, Mr. Jitters by name, didn't really live in Arrogancia. In fact, he lived on a small island close to the other side of the river. This island was famous for creatures who are brave and honest. Sadly though, one thing almost everyone knows about the blue and red trolls is that they are brave *except* around mice. They are unreasonably terrified of little mice.

It is legend that years and years ago, in the time of King Noble's great, great grandfather, the trolls of Arrogancia sailed across the river to the island and claimed it as their new home. To their surprise, a small kingdom of mice also lived on this island. There were more mice than any human could count on his fingers and his toes! At first the mice remained hidden, and the trolls had no idea of their presence. However, as time went on, mice began to peep out of holes in walls, in floors, and even in ceilings. Each time a little mouse would pop its head out, a troll would scream. Their lovely bright green fur slowly began to turn deep blue. Eventually, the mice disappeared—maybe due to all the screaming—but the fear the trolls had remained.

The trolls cried and cried. They missed their beautiful, emerald green fur. However,

as time went by, the island trolls became used to their blue fur, and they also came to understand how unpleasant it was to be scared. They didn't want to make anyone feel the way that the mice made them feel. The Troll Elders Council called an island meeting and established a rule—no more scaring. Instead, the island trolls would set out to make people laugh.

Unfortunately, Mr. Jitters wasn't always good at following the rules. Sometimes he would travel to Arrogancia and tell jokes to the people of the land, but most of the time, he would sneak across the river to pull pranks to give people just a *little* scare. Mr. Jitters forgot that people didn't like being scared either.

Chapter Five

"FIFTY-SIX, FIFTY-SEVEN, FIFTY...," Mr. Jitters counted out loud. "Oh, blast! I lost count!" Deciding that it was best to keep moving, Mr. Jitters stopped counting the brightly colored pebbles he passed. He needed to keep an eye out for the purple pebble. Keeping his eyes and mind on *purple*, Mr. Jitters searched high and low for this pebble. He passed through the Valley of Dancing Trees, over the Bridge of Silver Stone, and even managed to climb over the Wall of Frozen Water.

Because he had done so much walking, Mr. Jitters decided to take a break under a nearby tree. "I'm awful tired," Mr. Jitters said. "Maybe I can take a quick nap before I finish my search." As soon as Mr. Jitters closed his eyes, he heard a voice. "Sleeping on the job, are we?" the voice asked. Mr. Jitters' eyes flew open. He stood up so fast that he almost bumped into the king. The king began to laugh. "I'm sorry, Mr. Jitters. I didn't mean to startle you."

"King Noble, is that you?" asked Mr. Jitters, rubbing the sleep from his eyes.

"Yes, it is. What brings you to Arrogancia this time of year? I haven't seen you in months. The forests are full of mice, you know!" King Noble replied.

"I know, Your Majesty! That's why I traveled through the valley. I'm in search of the purple pebble," Mr. Jitters said proudly with a bow.

"Ah! I see. I suppose I should be searching for the pebble myself. However, there is a more important matter at hand. I seem to have lost

a chest full of gold. Have you seen it?"

Mr. Jitters thought for a moment and finally said, "No, sir, I haven't seen the gold. However, a knight and a pirate both saw your chest. The pirate told me that he was bringing it to you, but he dropped it on the road where the sun birds live."

"Oh, thank you for being so honest, Mr. Jitters!" the King exclaimed gratefully. "Good luck in your quest for the purple pebble." And with that, King Noble went in search of his chest.

Mr. Jitters felt glad that he had been honest and helped King Noble, but he still needed to find the pebble. He kept looking. He looked around every boulder and under every bush, but the pebble was nowhere to be found.

"Where oh where could this pebble be?" Mr. Jitters asked aloud. "It has to be here somewhere!" Just as he said that, he heard a loud rumble. Mr. Jitters jumped at the sound. Before he had a chance to realize what was going on, it started to rain. It wasn't a light rain either. It began to pour. Mr. Jitters' usually soft fur was now soaked and heavy. He saw several woodland creatures scurrying around. Nuts and berries they had just collected were being washed away by the rain.

"Oh no! All of our berries are gone. Now we're going to have to spend even *more* time collecting them all over again," cried a raccoon.

"I know! This is horrible!" complained a small squirrel.

Mr. Jitters couldn't help but smile. He refused to let rain ruin his day. Instead of crying and complaining, Mr. Jitters chose to do something better. He danced! He danced and danced until he was so dizzy that he fell over. Lying on the ground, Mr. Jitters laughed a loud and hearty laugh. He was so lost in his laughter that he laughed until the rain went away and the sun came out again.

Mr. Jitters stood up, shook his fur dry, did one more little dance, and then gathered all

the nearby nuts and berries and returned them to the woodland creatures. "Here ya go," Mr. Jitters said with a smile. "No need for crying and complaining." The woodland creatures smiled and thanked the little troll. With a light heart, Mr. Jitters continued his search for the purple pebble.

Mr. Jitters had such a good attitude that he couldn't stop smiling. To every creature he passed, he politely waved. And to every person, royalty or otherwise, that he saw, he bowed respectfully. *Maybe being kind and friendly is better than being mean and scary,* Mr. Jitters thought.

The sun was getting lower in the sky, and the air was getting cooler. Mr. Jitters had been searching almost all afternoon, and he still hadn't found the pebble. His legs were getting tired, but he was still smiling. "I think I need to rest for a bit," the tired troll confessed. Mr. Jitters went down to a small grassy area close to a stream. Lying on his back, he stared up

at the sky and watched the big, white, fluffy clouds as they floated across the late afternoon sky. He was just about to doze off for a little nap when he felt something tickle his feet. Mr. Jitters giggled a little bit, looked down, and let out a giant scream. "MOOOUUUUSEEEEE!" yelled Mr. Jitters. He had forgotten that Arrogancian mice love to relax by streams in the late afternoon.

"Ahhh! Get away! Get away!" Mr. Jitters continued to yell. The more he yelled, the more mice began to crawl around his feet. The terrified troll jumped up and down. Mr. Jitters was so scared that he couldn't listen. The mice tried to tell him that they weren't going to bother him. They just wanted to go for a swim, but Mr. Jitters didn't listen. He just continued to yell. All of his fur was standing on end because he was so scared. "Help!" Mr. Jitters tried to cry. But just as he got the word out, a giant net swooped down, picked him up, and, in a blink, dropped him next to Sir Liesalot and the pirate.

"What happened? Did you find the pebble?" the pirate asked.

"No...I...I...saw some little mice...and got scared. The net came and got me before I had the chance to run away...I'm sorry." Mr. Jitters said, his voice shaking.

"Oh no! Now what are we going to do? We have to get someone to find the pebble and wish us free. Otherwise, we'll be stuck here forever!" Sir Liesalot said.

The three began to lose hope. It seemed like there was no one who could help them get free. The pebble was nowhere to be found, and daylight was fading.

"Mateys, I really don't want to stay here overnight. I've got to get back to me crew!" the pirate groaned.

"I know, I know! Someone else has to come along. Practically everyone in the land is looking for this pebble. We just need to be patient," Sir Liesalot said.

A few crickets chirped, and the faintest

glow of a few early lightning bugs flashed amid the deep forest trees. Suddenly, Mr. Jitters' fur stood on end again. However, this time it was from excitement rather than fear! "Listen! Do you hear that?" Mr. Jitters asked.

"What? I don't hear anything," Sir Liesalot said.

"Shhhh...," the pirate urged. "I hear something. It sounds like singing."

Sure enough, coming down the road was a young girl. She looked to be about eight or nine years old. As she sang, she giggled. As she giggled, there was a light whistle that came from the small gap between her two front teeth, one of which was terribly loose.

"Hello!" the girl called out to the three as she came closer.

"Hello, little girl," the three said in unison.

"My name is Naya," she said as she smiled and curtsied.

"Nice to meet you, Naya." Mr. Jitters

responded. "I'm Mr. Jitters. May I ask what you're doing wandering alone so close to dark?"

"I'm in search of the purple pebble," Naya responded proudly. "But time is running out, so I have to find it fast!"

"Ah, I see," Mr. Jitters said.

"Yup! Wait a second, why are you guys stuck in place like that? Can't you move?" Naya asked, inspecting their feet.

"No, I'm afraid we can't," Sir Liesalot replied. "We were in search of the purple pebble too, but something happened to each of us on our quests, and a net swooped down and brought us back here."

"Oh!" Naya replied.

"Do you think you could help us get free?" asked the pirate.

"Well, I sure can try, but I need to find the purple pebble first. You see, I have this really important wish I need granted. I don't know if it will come true, but with the purple pebble, I think it could. Once I find it, I'll be sure to come back and help," Naya promised with a smile.

Her three new friends thought about it. If she didn't use her wish for them to be free, there was still a chance that they would be released after the pebble was found.

"All right, but please do come back here after you find the pebble, okay?" the pirate answered.

"I will. I promise!" Naya replied.

Chapter Six

NAYA WAS OFF ON her own adventure to find the pebble. She didn't have much time to find it. It was already late afternoon. She had to move quickly. She was determined to find the purple pebble before dark.

As Naya walked, she felt the late afternoon breeze. She pulled her jacket closer. The temperature was dropping. Even the trees seemed to be shivering. "I'm so thankful I'm wearing this jacket," Naya said and then began to sing,

"Even if it's cold, it's okay!
I have a jacket! La la la.

Even if it's cold, it's okay!
I have a jacket! La la la."

It seemed like everything was noticing Naya's good attitude. The trees shivered less, the wind calmed down, and the sun even seemed to rise a little higher in the sky. However, even though things were looking up, Naya still didn't see the purple pebble.

"Where on earth could it be? I've got to find it!" the girl mumbled to herself.

Naya continued to walk, keeping her eyes wide open as she did. If she saw anything that was shiny and purple, she stopped to see if it was the pebble. She wasn't having very much luck, but eventually, she came to the road that led to King Noble's castle.

"Why, hello there, little one!" the king called out.

"Hello, Your Majesty," Naya replied as she curtsied.

"What are you doing outside this late

in the day?" the king asked, his voice full of concern.

"I'm searching for the magical, purple pebble," Naya proudly said with a smile. "What are *you* doing?"

"Ah," King Noble paused. "I was looking for some of my gold. It was lost on a path a little way back, but I found it. Does your father know you're out here all alone?"

Naya hung her head. Truthfully, her father didn't know she was out. When he fell asleep for his afternoon nap, she slipped out to start her search. She didn't plan on being gone so long, but looking for the pebble was taking more time than she expected. The thought of being untruthful crossed Naya's mind. She didn't want King Noble to send her home. She had to find the pebble!

"No, Your Majesty," Naya said softly. "My father doesn't know I'm outside all alone."

"Well, young one, I truly admire your honesty, but I suggest you search quickly and get home as soon as possible. Before you know it, there will be nothing but the dim light of the moon and stars to guide you home." King Noble reached into his pocket and pulled out a small, square stone. "Here," the king said. "Take this stone. If it gets dark, shake it. The stone will turn a golden yellow, and it will light your pathway home." King Noble smiled and handed Naya his stone.

"Oh, thank you, sir!" Naya said. Now she was even more eager to keep looking for the pebble. In her heart, she knew the pebble was going to be found soon, and she just had an idea where to look for it next. She was so excited that she curtsied quickly, waved goodbye, and ran down a pathway toward The Rock Cave. This cave was known to be the home of a bear family.

Naya had never walked by The Rock Cave alone before, so she was a little nervous to do it now, but she didn't have a choice. She wanted to look for the pebble in the bushes with the beautiful pink and purple flowers, and the only place in all of the kingdom those bushes grew was just up the hill from The Rock Cave.

When she got close to the cave, she heard a strange sound. Several strange sounds actually. The bears were sleeping, and they were all snoring. The mother and father bears were asleep at the mouth of the cave with two cubs cuddled near them. Naya didn't want to wake the bear family, so she tiptoed quietly as she passed by. But just when Naya thought she was in the clear, a pepper fly flew in front of her face.

Pepper flies are some of the most annoying creatures in all of Arrogancia. It's almost impossible not to sneeze when they're around. As the fly passed her, Naya's nose began to itch and twitch. She could feel a sneeze coming. She tried to hold it in, because she knew that if she let it out, the bear family would wake up. *Ah...Ahh...AHCHOO!* Naya let out a giant sneeze. Her sneeze was so loud that it did indeed wake the entire bear family!

One by one, each bear raised its head. Naya stood very still, unsure what to do. She had heard the bears that live in this cave were pretty nice, except for when they were woken from their naps.

The mama bear let out a loud growl. Naya stood her ground. *Maybe if I just wait for all of them to growl at me, and I stay very still, the bears will calm down, and I can leave*, she thought. Each bear in the bear family took its turn growling at Naya, but she didn't move. She dug her feet into the grass and crossed her arms. The bear family looked at each other, and they all shrugged.

After a moment, they settled down again, ready to resume their naps. The youngest bear peeked at Naya and gave her a small bear smile. It was almost as if she was telling Naya that she was sorry for growling at her. Naya smiled back and gave the little bear a wink as she started on her way. After just a step or two, she already could hear the bear family snoring.

When Naya was finally far enough away that she couldn't hear the snoring anymore, she let out a deep sigh. "Boy!" she laughed. "I'm glad that's over. I guess that wasn't so scary after all." She started to sing again.

"Growling doesn't scare me, not today!
I'm gunna find the pebble. Hip hooray!"

Naya had such a good attitude. She knew she was getting closer to the pebble. Looking up, she noticed the sky was beginning to turn from a pretty blue with gold highlights to an orange and pink and deep blue. Soon it would be dark, and the moon would be out. "I've got to hurry!" Naya said. She looked behind trees and under rocks, but she still didn't see the pebble. "Where are you, purple pebble?" Naya sang.

Just then, Naya heard a little sound.

"Toodaloo!" She paused. She heard it again.

"Toodaloo! Toodaloo!"

The whistle was coming from the bushes with the beautiful pink and purple flowers!

"It's the pebble!" Naya squealed with delight. "I just know it is!" She ran to the bushes. There were so many beautiful flowers!

The funny whistling got louder and faster. "Toodaloo! Toodaloo! Toodaloo! Toodaloo!"

Naya searched and searched through the

flowers, but she didn't find the purple pebble. Naya said, "Oh my, how am I ever going to find the pebble among all the flowers, and now it's getting dark!"

That's when she saw them. She saw two eyes on a purple petal. They blinked. Naya carefully reached down and moved some of the little flowers out of the way.

"Toodaloo!" she whistled.

"Toodaloo to you too! You found me!" the purple pebble sang to her. The pebble hopped into Naya's hands, and she jumped for joy. She had done it! She had found the purple pebble!

Before Naya had time to think, in a blink, she was back in the familiar town square where Sir Liesalot, the pirate, and Mr. Jitters were waiting.

"Naya! You're back!" Mr. Jitters shouted.

"We were afraid you weren't going to come back," Sir Liesalot added a little shamefully.

"Yes, it's getting dark. All of the lamplights are turning on," the pirate said.

The little girl let out a small laugh and flashed a huge smile. "I promised I would come back!" she said. "And I found the pebble! I found the purple pebble!" Naya held out the small stone for the three to see.

"Ahhh!" they all said in unison. They couldn't believe it. After all of the searching they had done, this young girl had found the pebble.

Chapter Seven

DOOONG! THE SOUND RANG out. The grand search was over. Despite the evening hour, all the people of Arrogancia gathered by the clock tower where Naya, Sir Liesalot, the pirate, Mr. Jitters, and the pebble were. Naya found herself in the middle of a crowd.

"Weren't you scared?" "Was it hard to find the pebble?" "Where was it?" "How did you do it?" So many questions flew at Naya. She was a bit overwhelmed, but she was still so excited that she had found the pebble.

"What are you going to wish for?" someone asked. "She's just a young girl. What good could her wish do?" a certain princess added.

"Come now, child. Why don't you pass your wish along to someone else, hmm?" an officer advised.

A wish! Naya had almost forgotten all about her wish. She had gotten so caught up in all the excitement of finding the pebble that it had not yet sunk in that now she could make her wish!

"She's going to wish for us to be free!" Sir Liesalot said. Naya turned to look at her new friends. She did promise she would come back, but she never promised she'd wish for them to be free. She couldn't. She only had one wish, and it was really important. Naya's father was very sick. Unfortunately, her family did not have enough money to pay for him to go to the hospital. Naya figured that if she found the pebble, she could wish for her father to get better, and then her family wouldn't have to worry anymore.

Naya took a deep breath and let out a

loud whistle. Then she took a moment to wiggle her very loose front tooth. Her whistle was so loud that it got everyone's attention. All the people grew quiet and looked at Naya. She climbed up on the ledge surrounding the clock tower and stood under the words *Welcome to Arrogancia* carved in the stone.

Naya cleared her throat and spoke.

"Everyone! I have something to say. I have a wish to make. My daddy is very sick, and my family needs him to get better. So, I appreciate what you all have to say, but I wish for my daddy to get well."

Naya looked at the pebble in her hand. It started to shimmer and dance, and then it flew up into the air, leaving a trail of lovely purple dust and sparkles that lit up what was now a beautiful night sky. Then it was gone.

Everyone gasped, but before anyone could say a word, the pebble was back. It landed in Naya's hand and flashed her a big smile. Naya knew her wish had been granted.

She was so excited that she slipped the purple pebble into her coat pocket and sprinted for home to see her father.

Before she had gone too far, Naya remembered the stone King Noble had given her. She took it from her pocket, shook it, and held the stone in front of her. Its golden light lit the way as a smiling Naya ran as fast as she could. As she got closer to home, she could see the lamps were lit, and she could hear her family laughing together.

"Daddy! Daddy!" Naya shouted as she ran through the door. When she reached her father, he scooped her up in his arms and spun her around. "Where have you been, daughter?" he said.

"I'm sorry, Daddy," she replied. "But I found the magical, purple pebble and wished for you to be well! It worked! The pebble granted my wish!"

Naya's father let out a hearty laugh. "You did? Well, I'm glad you found it. I'm certainly

feeling much better! Now I know why! Thank you! But next time you decide to go on a grand adventure, tell your mother and me where you're going first, okay?"

"Yes, sir!" Naya said as she and her father hugged each other and laughed.

Naya, her father, and her family walked together to the clock tower. All of the people were still in the town square talking to each other. One thing had changed though. Sir Liesalot, the pirate, and Mr. Jitters were no longer stuck in place. When they saw Naya and her family, they ran to meet her.

"Naya!" they shouted in unison. "We're free!" They couldn't have been happier.

"I guess when you made your wish whatever was holding us in place let us go!" Sir Liesalot said.

"It's true," a small voice added. Naya looked down. It was the pebble talking. She pulled it out of her pocket. "When you made your one true wish, not only did it free your friends Sir Liesalot, the pirate, and Mr. Jitters but it freed the people of Arrogancia too." Naya looked confused.

"Freed the people? Freed them from what?" Naya asked.

"From all of their arrogance and pride. Everyone in the town was so touched by the selflessness of your wish, they realized it's better to be humble than arrogant," the pebble replied.

Naya looked around and saw all of the people had gathered around her and her family. They looked so happy and began to tell her how glad they were that her father wasn't sick anymore.

"Thank you for teaching us such important lessons!" a farmer said.

"Yes, thank you! We're sorry we let our arrogance get the best of us," responded a merchant.

"Naya, you were able to find the pebble because you are honest!" Sir Liesalot said. He walked over to the young servant he'd seen earlier in the day. "I'm sorry for lying to you. That wasn't very nice of me," Sir Liesalot said.

"And you had a good attitude!" added the pirate. "I'm going to try not to complain so much. It's no fun to be around someone who complains all the time."

"I agree," said Mr. Jitters. "Naya, you

were honest and had a good attitude *and* you were so brave too. I want to be more like that. I don't like being so scared when I shouldn't be, and I don't want to play tricks on people or scare them anymore."

Naya smiled and walked over to Mr. Jitters. She said, "I was scared on my adventure. It's okay to be scared sometimes. That's what my daddy taught me. Sometimes when we're scared, we have to keep going. That's what courage is!" Mr. Jitters gave Naya a big hug.

"And, Sir Liesalot, it's tempting to tell a lie sometimes, but wouldn't you agree it's much better to be honest?" asked Naya. Sir Liesalot didn't even have to think about it. He nodded with a smile.

"Yes, and it's way more fun to be around someone with a good attitude," added the pirate.

"Exactly!" Naya said.

King Noble placed his hand gently on Naya's head. "It would seem that you've taught some valuable lessons to the kingdom of Arrogancia, Naya. Indeed, just by being brave, honest, and kindhearted, you taught us so much."

Just then Naya had an idea. She whispered a moment to the pebble. It smiled and gave Naya a goodbye wink, then it flew up into the air again, leaving a new trail of purple dust and sparkles. The same gong sound that alerted the people of Arrogancia to the pebble's coming and going rang out again. There was a flash and everyone turned to the clock tower. The sign that once read "Welcome to Arrogancia" now read "Welcome to Humbleton"!

The End!

About the Author

JAYNA DUCKENFIELD is a proud graduate of Appalachian State University where she received a BA in English Literature. Having worked with children and young adults of all ages, her favorite stories are ones where kids and teenagers play the main role. In her spare time, you can find Jayna at Renovation Church, drinking dark roast coffee, or dancing around her living room in Atlanta, Georgia. This is her first book.

Made in the USA
San Bernardino, CA
01 December 2018